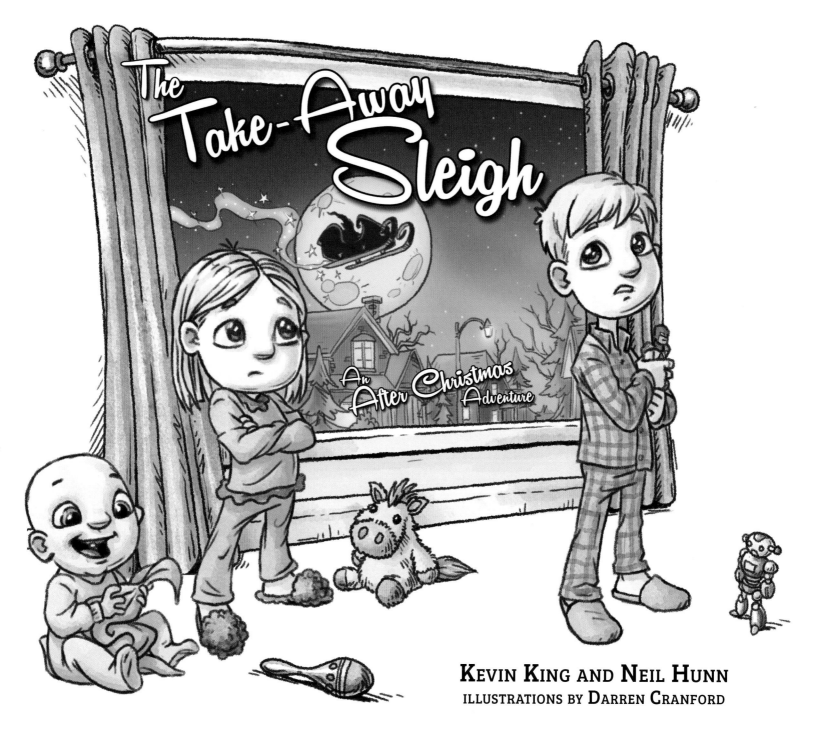

The Take-Away Sleigh

An After Christmas Adventure

KEVIN KING AND NEIL HUNN

ILLUSTRATIONS BY DARREN CRANFORD

TAKE AWAY SLEIGH LLC | LAKEWOOD RANCH, FL

Published by Take Away Sleigh LLC | Lakewood Ranch, FL
www.takeawaysleigh.com

Publisher's Cataloging-in-Publication Data
King, Kevin.

The Take-Away Sleigh : an after Christmas adventure / Kevin King and Neil Hunn ; illustrations by Darren Cranford. – Lakewood Ranch, FL : Take Away Sleigh LLC, 2020.

p. ; cm.

Summary: An after Christmas adventure that models good behavior and favorable results. Annie and Tommy learn a valuable life lesson about what it means to truly give.

ISBN13: 978-1-7351435-0-7

1. Christmas--Juvenile fiction. 2. Generosity--Juvenile fiction. 3. Gifts--Juvenile fiction. I. Title. II. Hunn, Neil. III. Cranford, Darren.

PZ7.5.K56 2020   2020910047
[E]--dc23

Project coordination by Jenkins Group, Inc.
www.BookPublishing.com

Printed in Korea by Pacom Korea, Inc., First Printing, July 2020, #34612-D7
24 23 22 21 20 • 5 4 3 2 1

Dedicated to Barb King

Fighting is naughty. We all know it's true.
But for Annie and Tommy, it's all they would do.
They fought over toys and TV and treats.
They fought in the car. "He's touching my seat!"

Finally their mother had more than enough.
She wanted her kids to share all their stuff.

"I'm done with this fighting. You know it's not right.
So the fighting is over on this very night."

"Santa rewarded the times you were good
And hoped you'd continue to do as you should.
So I've asked dear old Santa to come in his sleigh
To pick up your toys and take them away.

"For children who don't have the things we give you.
For children whose toys are all tattered and few."

"We'll be good," the kids promised.
"As good as can be,
The goodest of all, you just wait and see."

Mom shook her head. "You may beg all you like,
But the Take-Away Sleigh is coming tonight."

"Who knows what might go?" Annie said with a moan.
"The way we've been fighting, we'll lose all we own."

Mom left them to worry and mutter and fret.
To pace and to plan how to stop the sleigh yet.

"We'll pile up good deeds like logs in a stack.
If we're super good, the sleigh might turn back."

They filled up the day with good deeds galore,
With cleaning and helping and every good chore.

But though they were good, were they good enough?
Would this keep the sleigh from taking their stuff?

"Our fighting was naughty, and we did it a lot.
Have we done enough to make the sleigh stop?"

"What if we pick a toy for the sleigh?
One we won't miss when it's taken away."

So Annie rushed into her room in a jog.
She snatched up a toy that was chewed by the dog.

"For the sleigh," she told Mother. "This should be what we need.
To prove that today we are good kids … indeed."

"This old thing isn't giving," Mom said with a sigh.
"It's a toy. And I'm giving it. So tell me why?"

"When a gift is worth nothing, no goodness you've done.
What'er the sleigh takes, it won't be this one."

So Annie went to Baby and took her best toy.
A fluffy yellow bunny that gave her such joy.

"This bunny is special and should do the trick."
But Mother was grumpy at Annie's new pick.

"This bunny is Baby's. Take it back to her crib. You don't give a gift that's not yours to give."

"What can we do?" Annie howled to her brother.
"Every idea is bashed by our mother."

Tommy felt rotten with nothing to say
About all the trouble they'd made every day.
Now Mother was grumpy and Baby was sad.
And Annie was feeling so gloomy and bad.

"We could pick a good toy for the Take-Away Sleigh,
Something we really like and give it away.
I can give up the game that I got from Aunt Kate.
I've played it a lot and it's still pretty great."

"That's your favorite," said Annie, taken aback.
She couldn't imagine why Tommy would give that.

"That's why it's the best," Tommy said. "It'll do.
Now run and get something that's special to you."

"I don't think so," said Annie. "Your gift is enough
To stop that old sleigh from taking more stuff."

Tommy wanted to be the very best brother
So he took his good toy and gave it to Mother.

"The present you gave will make someone's day.
I'm so proud," Mother said in her happiest way.

Then Tommy was smiling and happy as well
And not a bit sorry... Annie could tell.
"This giving thing's funny. Why would Tommy feel joy
At giving away his favorite toy?"

She thought of some kids with nothing to do,
Not one single toy, or at least nothing new.
It must be just awful with no toys to play.
This thought made her fret the rest of the day.

She called to her mother just before bed.
"I have a good toy for the sleigh," Annie said.

Mom looked in surprise at the toy Annie clutched.
She could see it was something Annie loved very much.

"Tommy's gift made you happy. And he seems to feel glad.
I want that good feeling, 'cause I'm still feeling sad."

They put out the toys for the sleigh to collect
And dreamed of the kids their toys would affect.

Their mom was so proud she thought she might burst.
"Today ended the best, though it started the worst."

And then the next morning, they found something new.
Santa had left a surprise for these two.

A bright tiny sleigh waited right on the spot
To help them remember what they had been taught.

To be thoughtful and hopeful and kind to each other.
To do all their chores and to mind their dear mother.
For that is the hope of the Take-Away Sleigh
That goodness and giving will fill every day.

ABOUT THE AUTHORS

KEVIN KING and NEIL HUNN are brothers-in-law who were drawn to write this story to pay honor to Kevin's late wife, Barb. Barb and Kevin lived this story as they raised their three children in Cincinnati, Ohio.

Kevin now lives in Scottsdale, Arizona, and travels to be with his three adult children and grandchild.

Neil lives in Sarasota, Florida, with his wife and three children.

ABOUT THE ILLUSTRATOR

DARREN CRANFORD has illustrated more than 20 books and does concept art and storyboards for the movie and television industry as well as many other numerous commissioned works. Darren received his bachelor's degree in fine arts in Corner Brook, Newfoundland. He is the director and co-founder of Keyframe Digital Productions, Inc. Darren oversees the creative development and production of inspiring visual effects and animation for feature and broadcast television projects. With more than 20 years' experience, Darren's strength as an animation and VFX director as well as his storyboard expertise lends a unique eye to each book he illustrates. Darren recently directed 26 episodes of the second season of *Ollie: The Boy Who Became What He Ate* for CBC, was the animation supervisor for *Tee & Mo* for BBC, and has directed many internal animated projects.